MAY 0 9 2022

To my children, grandchildren,
and everyone else that gave GG
reasons to smile and be happy as
her Alzheimer's progressed.

ISBN: 978-1-7356410-4-1

First Paperback Edition, Febuarary 2022

Cover, Illustrations, Editing and Layout by Chris Dudley Art

Printed in United States of America

HD
HUDSON
DAWN
PUBLISHING

www.hudsondawnpublishing.com

GG Forgot My Name

Looking at Alzheimer's through the eyes of a four-year-old great-granddaughter, her brothers, and her cousins.

A Family Adjusting to Alzheimer's

Written by Cynthia Hughes
Illustrated by Chris B. Dudley

Hi! I'm Everly! These are my brothers Flynn and Declan!

We have a lot of cousins and all of us know we had the best great-grandma ever! We called her GG!

GG always made us feel special and happy, even when we were babies.

GG loved teaching us songs as she played the piano. We would smile and sing! GG made us happy and she was happy too!

One day, GG tried to play the piano for us, but she could not remember the songs. GG did not smile. She was not happy.

GG loved reading books to us. She made us laugh as she read using funny voices. GG made us happy and she was happy too!

One day GG tried to read a book to Declan, but she forgot some of the words.

GG did not smile. She was not happy.

I asked my Grandma why GG
could not read books or
play the piano like
she used to.

Grandma said that sometimes when people get older, they
get Alzheimer's. Grandma told me Alzheimer's made GG
forget a lot of things she used to know. GG would not like
this. GG would not be happy.

9

Grandma said that maybe it was time for us to make GG happy, just like she always made us happy. We did not want her to be sad about the things she forgot how to do.

10

We remembered how GG liked to sing songs with us, so we sang songs for her! GG clapped her hands and smiled. She was happy!

My cousin Colin remembered how GG loved to read books. One day he read six stories to GG at one time!

GG smiled. GG was happy.

GG liked to be outside. Colin's sister,
Charlie, liked to play outside with her.

GG made big bubbles. She smiled and was happy!

GG loved being with us at the river. Grandpa would take us for rides in the big four-wheeler with her! When we went down a big hill, GG would put her hands in the air and say, "Whee!" One day on our ride, GG told us that when she was a little girl she lived by a river. She said she liked to play in it with her brother!

14

I asked Grandma how GG could remember living by the river, but forgot a lot of other things. Grandma said that people with Alzheimer's, like GG had, could sometimes remember things from a long time ago, even if they forget a lot of things now. I was happy that GG could remember having fun with her brother.

Something else GG liked to do in the summer was to watch us swim in the pool. GG would say, "Nice job, Missy," "Nice job, Sissy," or "Nice job, Buddy." GG smiled. GG was happy.

I asked my Daddy why GG always called me Missy or Sissy, but never Everly. He said sometimes when a person has Alzheimer's, their brain changes and they cannot remember everyone's name.

Daddy said that even if GG forgets our names, she remembers we are someone very special to her and is always happy to see us.

We liked to be with GG even if she forgot our names.

GG smiled and was happy.

It was fun to talk with GG. When we talked to her, she would listen, smile and say, "Oh my!" She liked to spend time with us! GG smiled. GG was happy.

We all liked to FaceTime with Grandma and Grandpa,
so we could see GG. I would show GG what I learned
at dance class.

She would clap her hands and say, "Nice job, Sissy!"
GG smiled. GG was happy.

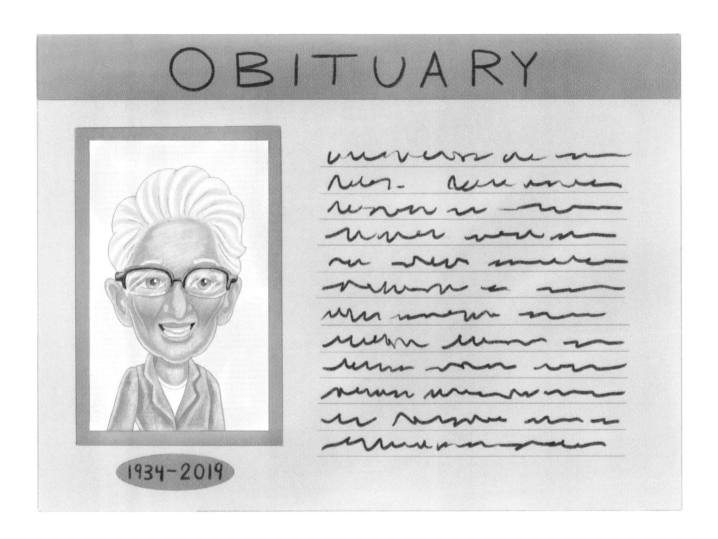

One day, Daddy told me GG had died. We told Grandma we were going to miss her. Flynn said he was sad he couldn't see GG anymore. Grandma said it was okay to miss someone when they have died because that means we loved them a lot.

Grandma said that every time we start to feel sad, we should remember something special about GG. Thinking about GG made us happy!

A few weeks after GG died, Grandma gave Charlie and me new baby dolls! Grandma said we could give our new baby a hug anytime we felt sad about missing GG.

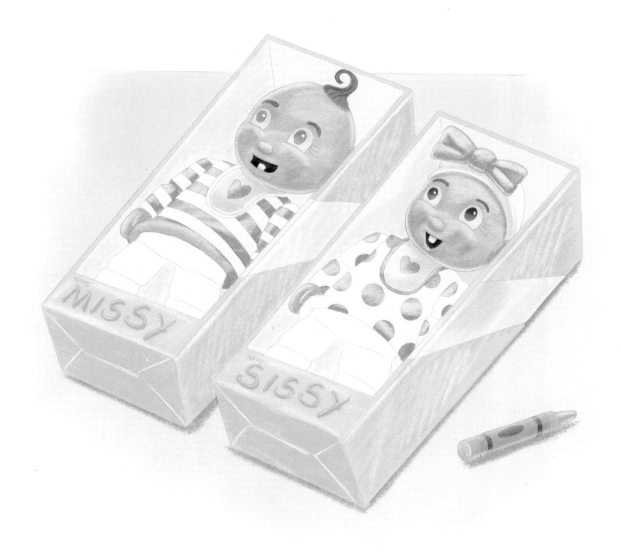

I told Charlie we should name our babies Missy and Sissy so it would be easy for GG to remember their names. GG would have smiled. GG would have been happy.

We gave our new babies a hug.

We smiled. We were happy.

GG will forever be in our hearts!